Time Goes By

A Day at a Zoo

Sarah Harrison

Ⓜ Millbrook Press / Minneapolis

First American edition published in 2009 by Lerner Publishing Group, Inc.

Copyright © 2005 by Orpheus Books Ltd.

Millbrook Press
A division of Lerner Publishing Group, Inc.
241 First Avenue North
Minneapolis, MN 55401 USA

Website address: www.lernerbooks.com

Library of Congress Cataloging-in-Publication Data

Harrison, Sarah, 1981–
    A day at a zoo / by Sarah Harrison.
        p.   cm. -- (Time goes by)
    Includes bibliographical references.
        ISBN 978-1-58013-554-2 (lib. bdg. : alk. paper)
    1. Zoo animals—Juvenile literature. 2. Zoos——Juvenile literature. I. Title.
    QL77.5.H27 2009
    590.73—dc22
                                                    2007045304

Manufactured in the United States of America
1 2 3 4 5 6 — BP — 14 13 12 11 10 09

Table of Contents

THIS IS THE STORY of a day at a zoo. All the pictures have the same view. But each one shows a different time of day. Lots of things happen during this single day. Can you spot them all?

Some of the same people and animals are on every page. Look for the zookeepers. They have a lot of work to do. Don't miss the two peacocks and the silly gibbons. Have you spotted the pickpocket? A tiny lizard is also in each scene.

You can follow the people and animals from morning until night. The clock on each right-hand page tells you what time of day it is.

While the zookeepers work, all sorts of other things are happening. Animals play and rest. Visitors come and go. People sell ice cream and hot dogs. There's always something new to find!

As you read, look for people who appear throughout the day. For example, some zookeepers always seem to be cleaning. Keep an eye on the veterinarian. Think about what stories these people might tell about the zoo.

Can you
find . . .

a bird?

The sun rises. Most of the animals are waking up. One of the tigers yawns. He shows his sharp, white teeth. The peacocks walk around freely. The giraffes look tired! But the raccoon has been awake all night. This animal is ready to sleep. Zookeepers look over each cage. They want to make sure the animals have fresh water. One worker says good morning to the gibbons. Other workers clean up.

6:00 A.M.

Waking up

A new arrival

The zoo opens

Feeding time

Escape!

A TV crew arrives

Closing time

Nighttime

a vet?

a garbage can?

Soon the first visitors will arrive. The people who sell hot dogs
and ice cream set up their stands. A worker opens the ticket booth.
A vet comes to check on the baby panda. A large van drives up.
The animals are very excited. Who could be inside? One of the
peacocks peeks at the new arrival.

8:00 A.M.

Waking up

A new arrival

The zoo opens

Feeding time

Escape!

A TV crew arrives

Closing time

Nighttime

Can you find . . .

a baseball cap?

an okapi?

a roller skater?

The zoo is open to the public. Everyone is eager to see the animals. The tigers are a little scary for some people! The gibbons make everyone laugh. Zookeepers take Sally, the friendly elephant, for a walk. Several people take photos of the new arrival. It's an okapi from Central Africa. Some children buy balloons that are shaped like their favorite animals.

10:00 A.M.

Waking up

A new arrival

The zoo opens

Feeding time

Escape!

A TV crew arrives

Closing time

Nighttime

a turtle?

a panda?

a zookeeper?

a dog?

It's time to feed the animals! The zookeepers give the penguins fresh fish. The pandas get bamboo shoots. The giraffes munch on green leaves. The gibbons can't wait to eat their lunch! The visitors are hungry too. A long line forms at the hot-dog stand. Some people go for ice-cream cones instead. Others share a picnic lunch on a bench.

12:00 P.M.

Waking up

A new arrival

The zoo opens

Feeding time

Escape!

A TV crew arrives

Closing time

Nighttime

a meerkat?

some balloons?

an escaped gibbon?

a hot-dog stand?

One of the gibbons has escaped! The zookeeper who fed them earlier left their cage door open. The naughty gibbon dashes around the zoo. He zips by visitors, sending hot dogs flying. The zookeepers quickly grab nets. They need to return the gibbon to the cage. At the same time, the vet keeps checking the animals. The giraffes and the pandas receive their weekly baths. Can you spot the pickpocket stealing someone's wallet?

2:00 P.M.

Waking up

A new arrival

The zoo opens

Feeding time

Escape!

A TV crew arrives

Closing time

Nighttime

Can you find . . .

a pickpocket?

a broom?

a baby ostrich?

a TV cameraman?

a large snake?

The zookeepers try hard to capture the escaped gibbon. But he doesn't want to go back to his cage. Soon a TV crew arrives. They will report on the exciting event. A reporter talks to the hot-dog seller to find out exactly what happened. Photographers take pictures of the other gibbons. A snake handler shows the visitors one of his largest snakes. They are allowed to hold it—if they feel brave enough.

3:30 P.M.

Waking up

A new arrival

The zoo opens

Feeding time

Escape!

A TV crew arrives

Closing time

Nighttime

Can you
find . . .

a peacock?

a man with an
umbrella?

a seal?

a schoolboy?

a penguin?

The zoo is about to close its doors. The visitors start to leave. But all of a sudden, the clouds darken. Rain pours down. Lightning flashes across the sky. People huddle under their umbrellas, trying to stay dry. One of the zookeepers falls into a puddle! The pandas take cover inside their home. But the seals and penguins enjoy themselves. They have fun getting wet and splashing one another.

6:00 P.M.

Waking up

A new arrival

The zoo opens

Feeding time

Escape!

A TV crew arrives

Closing time

Nighttime

Can you
find . . .

a flashlight?

a bat?

a tire?

a raccoon?

an owl?

a lizard?

20

The zoo is closed for the night. Darkness falls. Security guards patrol the grounds. They check that all the cages are locked. One of them finds two schoolchildren hiding in the meerkat pen. How long have they been there? The raccoon creeps out of its hut. It will stay awake all night. The other animals curl up and go to sleep. It is quiet at last. But where's the escaped gibbon?

9:00 P.M.

Waking up

A new arrival

The zoo opens

Feeding time

Escape!

A TV crew arrives

Closing time

Nighttime

Glossary

bamboo shoots: the young leaves of a woody, tropical grass called bamboo

gibbons: tailless apes that come from Southeast Asia

meerkats: animals from the mongoose family that come from southern Africa

okapi: an animal that is a cousin to the giraffe. Okapis come from Central Africa.

pickpocket: a thief who steals wallets and other items from people's pockets

seals: earless water animals that live in the ocean

security guards: people whose job is to protect people and animals from harm

vet: the short name for veterinarian, a doctor who cares for animals

zookeepers: people who take care of animals in a zoo

Learn More about Zoos

Books

Jarmin, Julia. *Class Two at the Zoo*. Minneapolis: Carolrhoda Books, 2007.

Kite, L. Patricia. *Racoons*. Minneapolis: Lerner Publications Company, 2004.

Levine, Michelle. *Giant Pandas*. Minneapolis: Lerner Publications Company, 2006.

Liebman, Dan. *I Want to Be a Zookeeper*. Richmond Hill, ON: Firefly Books, 2003.

Lowenstein, Felicia. *What Does a Veterinarian Do?* Berkeley Heights, NJ: Enslow Publishers, 2006.

Storad, Conrad J. *Meerkats*. Minneapolis: Lerner Publications Company, 2007.

Underwood, Deborah. *Colorful Peacocks*. Minneapolis: Lerner Publications Company, 2007.

Websites

Enchanted Learning

http://www.enchantedlearning.com

This fun website has all kinds of information, puzzles, and pages to color about many zoo animals.

National Zoo

http://www.nationalzoo.si.edu/Audiences/kids

This site features games, activities, quizzes, and more about the animals in the National Zoo in Washington, D.C.

A Closer Look

This book has a lot to find. Did you see people who showed up again and again? Think about what these people did and saw during the year. If these people kept journals, what would they write? A journal is a book with blank pages where people write down their thoughts. Have you ever kept a journal?

Try making a journal for one of the characters in this book. You will need a pencil and a piece of paper. Choose your character. Give your character a name. Write the time of day at the top of the page. Underneath, write about what the character is doing at that time. Pretend you are the character. What kind of work are you doing? Is your work hard or easy? What skills do you need to do the work? What have you noticed about the zoo? Have you seen anything surprising? What do you hope to do at work tomorrow?

Don't worry if you don't know how to spell every word. You can ask a parent or teacher for help if you need to. And be creative!

Index